This book
belongs to

LUCY

For my sisters, Christine and Elizabeth
T.B.

For Rach and Blueby
S.H.

First published in Great Britain in 2001 by

GULLANE
CHILDREN'S BOOKS

Winchester House, 259-269 Old Marylebone Road,
London NW1 5XJ

1 3 5 7 9 10 8 6 4 2

Text © Tony Bonning 2001
Illustrations © Sally Hobson 2001

The right of Tony Bonning and Sally Hobson to be identified
as the author and illustrator of this work has been asserted by them
in accordance with the Copyright, Designs and Patents Act 1988.

A CIP record for this title is available from the British Library.

ISBN 1-86233-322-X hardback
ISBN 1-86233-436-6 paperback

Printed and bound in China

Stone Soup

Tony Bonning

Illustrated by Sally Hobson

GULLANE
CHILDREN'S BOOKS

One afternoon, a tired and hungry fox stopped at the farm gate.

"Can you spare a little food for a hungry traveller?" he asked.

"No!" said Cow.
"I don't have any extra," said Donkey.
"Not me," said Goat.
"No! No! No! No!" said the four hens.
"Go away!" said bad-tempered Old Dog.

"Well, may I trouble you for a drop of water
to make some soup?" asked Fox.

Sheep, who was kinder
than the others,
brought some
water in a bucket.

Fox lit a fire, took a pot
from his backpack,
poured in the water
and put it on the fire.

Soon the water was bubbling away.

Carefully, Fox chose a stone, sniffed it, and dropped it into the water. "That should make a fine pot of stone soup," he said.

Full of curiosity, the animals gathered closer as Fox took a spoon from his bag, dipped it in the water and had a taste. "Mmm! Lovely!" he said. "But it's not quite right."

"I think it could do with a touch of salt and pepper. Do you have any?" he asked Sheep

Sheep fetched some salt and pepper and Fox put it in the pot.
The puzzled animals moved closer as Fox took a sip.

But still the soup wasn't quite right.

Fox thought perhaps
a taste of turnip might do it.
Cow went to her shed, chose
a turnip and gave it to Fox, who
chopped it up and put it in the pot.
Fox took a long sniff and a small sip . . .

But still the soup wasn't quite right.

Fox wondered
if a hint of carrot
would do the trick.
Donkey knew just
where to find one and
trotted off to get it.

He came back with a large carrot which was also chopped up and dropped into the pot . . .

But still the soup wasn't quite right.

Fox thought something was missing . . .
Of course! It needed a cabbage!
Goat hot-trotted off to get one.
By now the animals were leaning right over
the steaming pot, their mouths watering . . .

But *still* the soup wasn't quite right.

Fox was sure a sprinkling of corn
would be the finishing touch.
The hens dashed away and rushed back with
bowls of corn which were also tipped into the pot.

The soup bubbled and boiled,
and the animals licked their lips.

At last, the stone soup was just right, and they all shared it . . . down to the very last, delicious drop.

Everyone agreed it was the best soup they'd
ever tasted. Even Old Dog said so. "And all
from a stone!" he said.
"Amazing," they all agreed.

"Well, time to go," said
Fox, putting on his backpack.
All the animals wished him luck and
told him to stop and make another pot
of stone soup if he ever passed the farm again.
"Thank you," said Fox, with a wily smile. "I certainly will."

And he set off, down the road.

Other Gullane Picture Books
for you to enjoy:

I'm a Tiger Too!
MARIE-LOUISE FITZPATRICK
hardback: 1 86233 234 7
paperback: 1 86233 309 2

Lucky Socks
CHARLOTTE MIDDLETON
hardback: 1 86233 258 4
paperback: 1 86233 398 X

Sometimes I Like to Curl up in a Ball
VICKI CHURCHILL • CHARLES FUGE
hardback: 1 86233 253 3
paperback: 1 86233 396 3

Three Little Kittens
TANYA LINCH
hardback: 1 86233 204 5
paperback: 1 86233 314 9

GULLANE
CHILDREN'S BOOKS